Have Courage My Love

by Lisa Hewitt-Savelli
Illustrations by Daniel Gauthier

Somewhere, high in the sky lives a small cloud named Ben. Usually, you can see him gliding playfully behind his mother.

With his mother's encouragement he likes to explore and discover the world around him.

Ben hopes to grow strong like his mother. Like a fierce wind, she can be powerful and determined. Yet, like a gentle breeze, she is comforting and tender. Especially, when she says the words " I believe in you." Hearing these words gives Ben courage and makes him feel happy and warm inside.

One hot summer afternoon, Ben's mother noticed him floating lazily behind her and on his cute little face he wore a big pout. "Ben, why are you pouting?" she asked.

"I'm bored," he whined.

"Why don't we go for a ride?" she suggested happily.

"Naaa, I don't feel like it," he replied.

"Do you want to visit your friends on the farm?" she asked. "Naaa, I don't feel like it," he said with frustration.

B en thought for a moment, "What if I fly higher into the sky? I've never gone there before."

Now Ben became excited. With a big grin he told his mother where he wanted to go. He was sure that he was big enough and that he could keep himself safe. Ben's mother trusted him. She believed that he was ready to do some things on his own. Together they made some rules. He was not to go farther than the barn and no higher than the mountain top. Of course, he had to be back before dinner.

"I'll be fine," Ben shouted back to his mother. Although his stomach began to feel queasy, he told himself that he was not scared. He had courage.

Just then, an unexpected gust of wind blew Ben off course. In seconds, he found himself among a group of clouds much larger than he. One of the strange clouds came up to him. He asked Ben if he wanted to play with him and his friends.

Ben looked at the strange cloud and thought to himself, "He sounds like a nice cloud and he looks strong and powerful, just the way I want to be when I get bigger." Ben quickly looked at the other clouds. They all seem to be his friends. But, something didn't feel right. His stomach felt upset and queasy. His heart felt like it was running a race. Suddenly, he began to sweat. "Maybe I should return home?"

"Naaa, I'm ok!" he tried to assure himself. Ignoring his feelings, Ben smiled and said out loud, "Sure, I'll hang out with you and your friends."

"Great!" said the strange cloud. "We are just about ready to go," he snickered.

Avery

Like a powerful vacuum cleaner the strange cloud quickly sucked Ben up and away they flew. He dragged Ben up higher into the sky, far away from his home.

"Hey!" Ben yelled, "I can fly as fast as you." Ben struggled to break himself free. "You don't have to drag me," he persisted. But his new friend would not listen to him.

"You have to follow me and do what I tell you to," the new friend yelled back. Then he shouted out at the sky, "I'm the most powerful because everyone listens to me." Ben saw that all the clouds laughed nervously when his powerful friend spoke.

Ben struggled again to free himself, but he just wasn't strong enough. He felt powerless compared to his new friend. This was not fun! Ben realized that his stomach was telling him that he felt scared and did not trust this strange cloud. Ben started to panic and his eyes quickly filled with tears.

"Ah, look at the little cry baby!" the strange cloud snickered.

And right before Ben's eyes the strange cloud grew bigger and bigger, until he was huge. Ben felt small next to the giant cloud and helpless as he dragged Ben higher into the sky.

"Is this cloud my friend or does he just want to control me?"
Ben thought.

The giant cloud ordered all th
Ben's surprise, they all did wh
giant storm cloud. Ben had nev
he continued to feel trapped an
when they saw Ben crying.
strength, but he still could n

ouds to band together. And to
told them. This formed one
en the sky so dark. Startled,
elpless. Together, they all laughed
ustrated he pulled with all of his
reak himself free.

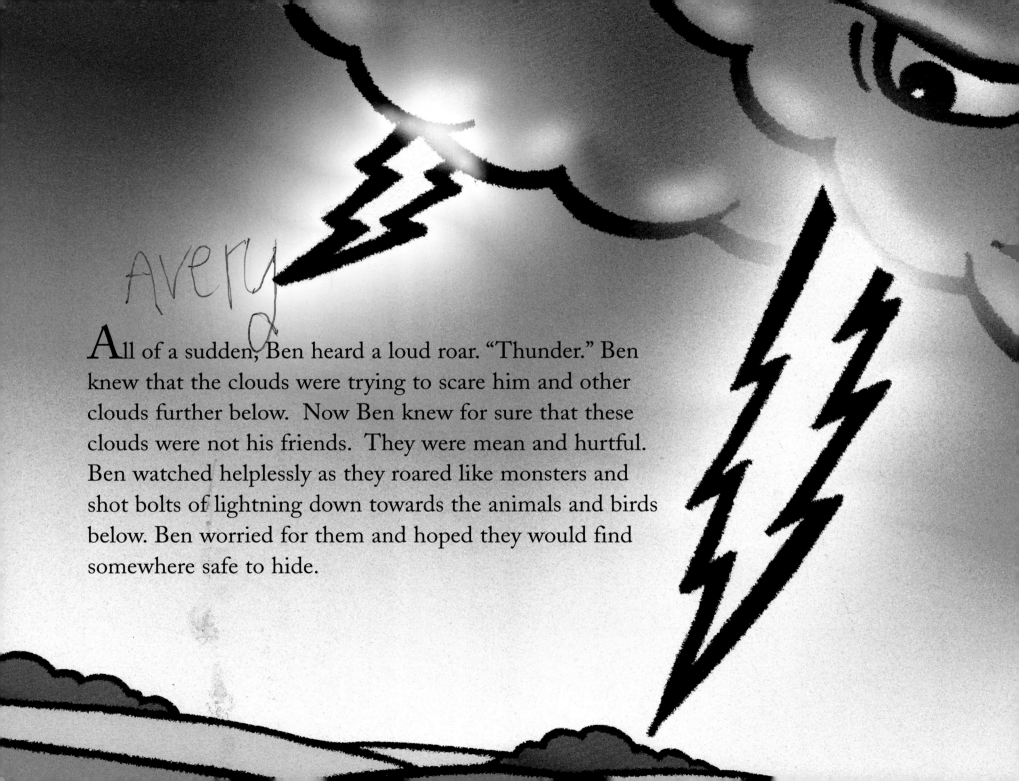

Avery

All of a sudden, Ben heard a loud roar. "Thunder." Ben
knew that the clouds were trying to scare him and other
clouds further below. Now Ben knew for sure that these
clouds were not his friends. They were mean and hurtful.
Ben watched helplessly as they roared like monsters and
shot bolts of lightning down towards the animals and birds
below. Ben worried for them and hoped they would find
somewhere safe to hide.

Avery

Ben had to do something. He knew he could not stop the big storm clouds. But he did not have to be part of them. He wanted to be himself again. He would have to pull himself free, but how?

Ben tried to think. "What can I do? I'm too small. I'm too weak. I'm powerless against them." Ben felt defeated, then suddenly he heard his mother's gentle voice say; *"I believe in you, Ben. You must believe in yourself.*

HAVE COURAGE MY LOVE, YOU CAN DO THIS!"

Avery

Ben flew back home. He was excited to tell his mother of his adventure. Ben told her where he had gone and what had happened.

She hugged him and whispered, "I'm so proud of you, you believed in yourself. You are a brave young cloud."

Ben beamed with delight, he felt so proud of himself. Finally, inside his stomach he felt wonderful and calm.

From that day on Ben grew to be a confident cloud, flying through the sky. He had learned how to trust and listen to his feelings. Today, Ben flies high above the mountains. He is a strong and wonderful cloud. He has many friends, because he believes in himself.

Avery

Getting to know your child better...

Have Courage My Love is a book about self-esteem, bullying, friendship, peer pressure and making tough choices. Children may find it difficult to talk about these issues. After reading the story, you may want to encourage discussion with your child(ren).

The questions and tips below may be used to encourage conversation with your child? Choose those which are right for both you and your child.

Encourage your child(ren) to share their experience(s) with you. You may want to phrase your questions so that you trigger their memory. For example: Whom did you play with during recess today? Did you have fun?

Think of your friends:

• What do you like best about them?

• What do you like least about them?

• If one of your friends asked you to do something that made you feel uncomfortable, what would you do?

• What do you think about a friend who says, "I'll only be your friend if…"?

• Do you think that people sometimes pretend to be friendly?

• Have you ever pretended to be happy when you really felt scared or unsure?

• How do you feel when you try new things? (Give your child examples like trying a new sport, starting a new school, making new friends etc…)

• What do you like best about yourself?

• Do you have a story of courage like Ben that you want to share?